Hiding Out

HIDING OUT

By Thomas Rockwell

Illustrated by Charles Molina

BRADBURY PRESS / SCARSDALE, NEW YORK

Hiding Out

When Verny asked me about Mom, I turned around and looked at him. "Is she what?" We were following an overgrown road through the woods on Red Mountain. His father'd let us off just across the state line in Massachusetts that morning so we could hike back along the ridges.

"Is she going to marry Mr. Wilson?" he said. He started around me. "Come on, let's get going."

"What would she want to get married for?" I said.

"I don't know. I just heard my mother telling somebody on the phone last night."

"No," I said.

We kept on up the road. Mr. Wilson? "You mean the man who runs Saylor's horse farm?" I said.

"I don't know. I suppose so. I wasn't really listening."

I couldn't get it through my head. I don't know, I guess I'd just never thought about Mom getting married again. Then I remembered a couple of nights before, Mom had had to go to a meeting after supper at the

1

Weeks's house, so Joe and Susie and me had
washed the dishes and then waited for her
out front. But when she'd finally come downstairs and I'd started out the gate, she'd said,
No, not yet. So we'd waited, and pretty soon
Mr. Wilson had come along with his two
daughters, Anne and Mary, and we'd all
gone off together, Mom and Mr. Wilson
walking ahead.

I started to ask Verny who his mother'd
been talking to, but then I stumbled up
against him.

"Look." He was pointing ahead through
the trees.

A field of grass dipped out of sight, then spread up to the forest line again, three or four hundred yards away.

"A field?" I said. "Way up here on the mountain?"

"And see the house? Just poking up behind that dip?"

"Come on."

We ran up the road and out into the field. A tumble-down, weather-beaten house in the long yellow grass—the front porch sagging, the roof falling in, most of the windows busted out.

I grabbed Verny. "Suppose someone still lives there?"

We knelt in the grass, watching the house.

"Come on," said Verny. "How could anyone live there? There isn't even a path through the grass to the porch."

But it was sort of eerie, even though the sun was shining and the wind hissing through the grass and rustling in the leaves in the woods behind us—that tumble-down, gap-windowed house sitting there in the old meadow way up on Red Mountain. There was a lopsided armchair on the porch, weeds growing out of the seat.

"Yeah," I said, "but look at the shack old

Hoddy Turner lives in. It isn't any better."

"But nobody'd live way up here on the mountain," said Verny. "Did you ever hear of anybody living way up here?"

"What difference does it make if we wait five minutes?"

I could just see us pushing open the door and some crazy, shaggy old man jumping out at us.

So Verny sat back cross-legged, grumbling, and rummaged in his knapsack for something to eat. A bird flew out of a hole in the roof of the house.

"I'm gonna crawl around to the other side," I said. "Maybe there's a path in from there."

I crawled off through the grass. I still couldn't figure it out about Mom. She was always telling us she didn't want us to forget our father. She kept his picture by the telephone in the kitchen; she'd tell us stuff about him. But now she was forgetting him, wasn't she? . . . The worst thing was I knew Mr. Wilson's wife had died just like my father had. Verny'd told me once after Mr. Wilson had given us a ride up from the Sandgate Road . . . I couldn't remember what him and Mom had talked about walking to the meeting. I hadn't noticed him coming around the house any more than Mr. or Mrs. Weeks or Mrs. Stanner lately.

Verny was calling me. I stood up.

"Come on. There's no one here."

He waited by the porch till I came up to him. "Geez, you know you crawled almost the whole way around."

"I didn't see any paths," I said.

The porch steps had fallen in; the front door was half open. I could see sunlight slanting into a corner of the room, probably from the hole in the roof. We climbed up on the porch and looked in the windows—a table and some broken chairs, plaster from the ceiling heaped all over everything. Verny set his knapsack down and pushed gently at the door. It was stuck. He edged in, peering around the door into the blind side of the room.

"Nothing but junk," he said.

I looked in over his shoulder. There was a sink against the back wall, beside it an empty space where a stove must have stood. I could see sunlit grass through the cracks in the door to the back shed. Overhead in the attic something rustled, a bird cheeped. We both started and then grinned at each

6

other. I went over and opened the cabinet above the sink; Verny looked up the stairway against the side wall.

"Nothing here," I said.

"Come on. Let's go up into the attic."

There were a couple of wooden trunks, heaps of rubbish from the roof, old clothes strewn about. Verny poked in one of the trunks with a broken lath. I squeezed past him. Sunlight streamed through the holes in the roof; birds were cheeping in a nest under the eaves. I kept listening for any sounds from downstairs, glancing out the window frame at the deserted field.

"Hey. I found something."

Verny squatted over a wooden box he'd uncovered. "It's an old chemistry set."

The scales were rusty; some of the little wooden chemical jars had rotted; the labels had faded and run. The set had probably lain there in the rain and snow for years. Verny shut it up.

"I'm taking it."

"What'll your father say? Suppose he makes you bring it back?"

"Naw. If we left it here, it'd just rot. Come on, maybe there's other stuff."

So we poked around some more. Verny

found a box of old buttons. I kept wondering what had happened to the people who'd lived in the house, whether they'd all died suddenly or something. Maybe just the boy they'd bought the chemistry set for had died, but then his mother hadn't wanted to live there anymore so they'd shut up the house and gone away. Or maybe the parents had died, and relatives had come and taken the kids. After my father died, I worried a lot about what would happen to Joe and me if Mom got sick or something. I remember sitting on the back steps wondering about my two aunts, who I'd seen at the funeral— trying to imagine what their husbands looked like, what kind of houses they lived in ...

Verny was muttering to himself, the birds cheeping in the eaves; I could hear a bush scraping against the side of the house in the wind ...

Why couldn't things stay just like they were? Mom fixing dinner when I brought Joe and Susie home from school. We'd all wash up, telling her what we'd done that day. Then she'd dish up the plates, and I'd put them around at the places. If it was winter, it'd be dark already, the wind sighing around the house maybe, and Mom would

leave the oven door open so we'd get a little more warmth in the kitchen . . .

"Come on," said Verny. "There's nothing more up here."

We edged back down the rickety stairs. I hadn't minded the lonely, rubbishy room before, the cupboard door hanging open, the empty space where the stove had stood, but now, I don't know, it all looked sort of dismal. Verny began to poke around in the corners. I went out onto the porch and watched the wind waving and waving through the yellow grass.

"There's a cellar," said Verny from inside "Hey, Billy, come look."

He was kneeling over a trapdoor unde the table.

"You can't see anything much," he said.

I got down on my hands and knees besid him.

"If we only had a candle or something, he said.

I spit down into the darkness. "It's no very deep."

"Come on," he said, backing out from ur der the table. "We'll make a torch. I'll win my T-shirt around a stick."

When we got the torch smoldering, he la down on his stomach and reached it as fa

9

as he could down into the cellar. It was only about four feet deep, gobs of cobwebs hanging from the ceiling, a dirt floor, piles of rusty old tin cans.

"You want to go down?" Verny said.

"There's nothing down there."

"Every time they finished a can of beans or something, they must have just opened up the trapdoor and chucked it into the cellar."

"Yeah. Come on. Let's go."

Out on the porch Verny stuffed the chemistry set into his knapsack. I picked up a rusty hammer head for a souvenir. At the edge of the woods I looked back at the deserted, tumble-down house.

"I wonder who could have built it?" I said. "Way up here on the mountain, ten or twelve miles from anybody else?"

Verny shrugged. We set off through the woods.

When I got home that night Mrs. Stanner was there, babysitting; Mom had gone out. So I said goodnight and went upstairs and woke Joe and told him what Verny had said. Then I got him to promise he'd ask Mom at breakfast if she was going to marry Mr. Wilson.

"Who told you that?" she said.

"No one," said Joe. "I just wondered. He came with us the other night to the Weeks's."

She didn't answer. She had on her old blue bathrobe; her hair hung loose onto her shoulders. She had to keep brushing it away from her face with the back of her hand while she stirred the oatmeal. I watched her. She didn't act any different than she always had.

But that afternoon—it was Sunday—Mr. Wilson came over and she and him wandered around the yard, talking, while she showed him her flowers. He didn't say much. I finally got so fed up I kicked the porch steps and went out through the house and wandered along by the river. Why did she want to marry him? He didn't even have a house like we did; he just rented part of the Simmons'. He drove this rattly old Chevy, the back seat cluttered with harness and junk, tools and greasy rags stuck up on the dashboard.

After a while I went over to Verny's and asked him if he'd ever run away.

"What do you want to run away for?" he said.

He was sitting on his back porch eating a chicken-salad sandwich.

"Who said I did?"

"Then why'd you ask me if *I* ever had?"

I shrugged and sat down on the porch steps.

"It's because your mother's really getting married, huh," he said after a while.

I didn't say anything.

"You want a sandwich?" he said.

I shook my head. After a while he said, "I could never figure out where to run to. I thought any place I went, they'd probably find me and bring me back. And I figured when I got hungry, I'd probably come back anyway, so what was the use?"

He went into the house and came back with two pieces of chocolate cake. After I'd finished the cake, I got up and said I had to go.

"You still coming hunting tomorrow?" he said. "Ma says she'll fix us lunch."

So I nodded, and he said he'd come by for me early, and I went off. I felt so tired, I wanted to just lie down anywhere and never get up. I don't know. I couldn't stop thinking about Mr. Wilson coming downstairs every morning while Mom was cooking breakfast in her bathrobe. Probably he'd make me work up at the farm all the time. At night he'd sleep in her bedroom.

When I got home, Anne and Mary were there, and Mom wouldn't let me go up to my room even when I whispered to her I had a stomach ache. Afterwards she told me I hadn't been polite enough, she didn't ever want to hear me speak to Anne and Mary that way again.

"Why should I be politer to them than anyone else?" I said.

"Don't talk to me like that," she said. "You heard me."

"What did I say to them? What? I only

said Verny and me were going off by ourselves tomorrow. What's wrong with that?"

But I knew all right. Mary, the oldest one, had asked me if I wanted to go picking blueberries with them the next day. I figured Mr. Wilson and Mom had put her up to it, trying to get all of us to act like brothers and sisters, so I'd said, Naw, Verny Stillwell and me were going somewhere by ourselves.

Next morning before the sun was up, Verny rattled some pebbles off my window, and I crawled over Joe and grabbed my clothes and snuck out onto the back porch.

"What'd your mother pack for lunch?" I whispered.

While Verny showed me—fried chicken and thick ham sandwiches and slices of apple pie and gingerbread and two bottles of orange soda—I hopped around the porch pulling on my clothes. It was cold with the sun not up yet; my legs were all goose pimples. But the birds were peeping and whistling and chattering like they always do just before dawn, and Verny'd brought his 22 and there wasn't a cloud in the whole sky, just an orange glow spreading up over the mountains back of Catersville and the last stars winking out beyond Carlisle. So I began to feel pretty good, and tying my sneakers, watching Verny pack the lunch back into his knapsack, I said to myself, The heck with it. I won't think about it *once* today. What do I care? I can always figure something out.

"Ready?" said Verny, heaving his knapsack back on.

So we set out, climbed over the back fence and slogged down through the meadow toward the mist drifting in the fields by the river. Before we'd gone ten feet our sneakers and pants were sopped. Pretty soon we came to the first low-lying wisps and then the gray mist was all around us; we couldn't see three feet ahead or hear anything except the wet hay swushing against our pants and now and then a rabbit suddenly starting up nearby and bounding away. We went single file, Verny in front because he had the gun, heading toward the river. It was real eerie, so still. Like the upper reaches of the Zambezi, maybe.

"You sure we're headed right?" I said after a while. I almost jumped at the sound of my own voice, it sounded so loud in the mist.

Verny looked back. Little droplets of mist clung to his hair and eyebrows. He'd wrapped his handkerchief around the bolt of his gun to protect it.

"Sure."

"How can you tell?"

"We were headed right when we went into the mist, and I've been walking straight ever since."

"Yeah, but sometimes if you're not sighting on a tree or something, you can be walking in circles even when you think you're walking straight. We should have got to the river before this."

"Naw. Come on. The mist makes you think we've been walking longer than we have."

So we went on and pretty soon Verny stopped and said, "Listen."

And sure enough, I could hear the dim splash and gurgle of rapids ahead, and a few minutes later we came out on the bank of the river. But it turned out we'd both been right, because we hit the river but too far downstream.

We waded across, carrying our sneakers, and followed a cowpath up the mountain through the dripping underbrush. Pretty soon we could see the sun burning through the mist overhead like a light bulb. At the top of Bleecker's hill-meadow we came out of the mist and stopped to look back. It stretched all the way to Bonville, dazzling white in the sunshine, hillocky and still, nothing showing but a treetop here and there.

Verny wiped off the 22 and loaded it, and we crawled under the fence and started up the stone wall running into the woods, going real quiet.

Pretty soon Verny stopped still, but I couldn't see anything, and then he raised the gun slowly, sighting it, and I spotted the chipmunk's head poking out between two rocks . . . *Blam!* . . . Then silence, the echo fading away . . . A faint scrabbling in the wall died away . . .

"D'you hit him?" I whispered.

"I think so."

We edged closer, craning our necks to look.

"You see him?"

And then Verny pointed, and I saw the chipmunk on his back between two stones. Verny lifted him out by the tail and laid him on a rock, and we squatted down, looking at him.

"You got him right in the neck."

"It probably broke his backbone so he never even knew what hit him."

Verny handed me the gun and got out his hunting knife and, pressing the chipmunk down on the rock with a stick, cut off its

tail. Then we went on, me in front now because it was my turn to shoot. By the time we'd worked our way to the ridge, we'd each shot two. One we had to dig out of the wall, and when we finally got to him, rocks scattered all around behind us, he was still breathing; Verny had to shoot him again. The bullet flipped him right off the wall into the weeds, ripping his stomach all open.

18

When we came to the top of the ridge, we set the gun and knapsack by a fencepost and began picking blueberries. Every summer the town had a fruit stand down on the Sunderland road on weekends. All of us kids were supposed to pick at least three quarts of berries a week.

"When'll we eat lunch?" Verny said after a while from behind a bush.

"We better not till after we've been to the stand," I said. "Mrs. Weeks told me she'd need the berries by noontime."

"Geez," said Verny.

So we picked along up the ridge, the sun getting hotter and hotter. Verny tied his handkerchief around his forehead to keep the sweat out of his eyes. We both took off our shirts. When we'd filled our pails twice, we sat down under a bush and drank some of our soda and ate our pieces of pie. Verny's mouth was all purple from eating berries.

"You'll make yourself sick eating all those berries," I said.

"Naw," he said. "I never get sick from eating."

So we went back to picking. By the time I'd picked my three quarts, the sun was almost straight overhead. Verny still had a way to go because he'd been eating so many. So I set my berries in the shade of the knapsack and went off down the wall with the 22 to see if I could get a shot.

Pretty soon I heard a chipmunk chirp somewhere ahead of me, but I couldn't locate him in the checkered sunlight and shadows of the woods. I tried to creep nearer, but everytime I got close, he'd chirrup and run further down the wall. He didn't act scared or anything; I figured he was just scampering along looking for stuff to eat.

The woods felt cool and fresh after picking berries all morning, bent over in the hot sun; I could smell the moss and rotting tree stumps; every so often I'd get a whiff of the sun-hot, tindery berry bushes back on the ridge. Pretty soon I quit stalking the chipmunk and sat down on a rock . . . Then I saw him, perched on an old stump about ten feet from me. So I raised the gun slowly, not even moving my head, and fired. He froze; I'd missed him. So I reloaded, not taking my eyes off him, and fired again. He still didn't move. He was clutching a seed in his forepaws. I fired again. He stared at me, nose twitching. I edged forward and fired again. I couldn't have been more than six feet from him. My hands were trembling so I could hardly load. Why didn't he run? I didn't even want to shoot him anymore. *Why didn't he run?*

Then all of a sudden Verny was panting beside me, asking, What was I shooting at, for cripes sake? I was wasting all the bullets.

So I looked at him and then back at the stump, and the chipmunk was gone.

"It was a chipmunk," I said, lowering the gun. "I kept missing him."

"On that stump?"

Verny went over and looked behind it.

"You got him."

He held up the chipmunk to show me and then laid him on the stump. "You used enough bullets."

I went over and looked at the chipmunk —its tiny claws, the soft white fur on its belly. I couldn't figure out why I hadn't let him go, why I hadn't just stopped shooting. It made me feel sort of sick to my stomach. Why hadn't he run? I don't know, I almost felt like crying.

"Why didn't he run?" I said.

"He froze," Verny said, as if he knew all about it. "He got so scared he froze."

So we went back up on the ridge, and I

sat by the knapsack while Verny finished picking. I still couldn't get the thing straight in my mind. I couldn't figure out why the chipmunk hadn't run, or why I hadn't just turned and walked away; it sort of scared me. And then I got to thinking about Mom and Mr. Wilson. I could see us all sitting at the table having dinner, none of us saying anything, just eating and eating. Going down to the stand, I just tramped along behind Verny, watching his sneakers scuff ahead of me through the leaves.

When we got to the stand, Mom was there with Joe and Susie and Mrs. Weeks. Verny sat right down under a tree and began to eat his lunch, but I didn't feel like eating so I just hung around while Mom dumped our berries into the big strainer they used for washing and culling, and then helped her carry it down to the stream. She set it in the stream and rolled up her sleeves and I took off my sneakers and socks and waded in, and we culled and washed the berries together. She did most of it, though, because I kept stopping to watch her. I couldn't figure out how her hands could work so fast, swirling the berries around in the water, culling out green and mashed ones, scooping up handfuls of good ones into the pail on the bank beside her, swirling the berries around again, her hands dead white in the cold water and swimming blueberries. By the time she'd finished and turned the strainer over, banging it on the bottom to knock the leaves and stems and stray berries out of it, I'd forgot about the chipmunk. When we got back to the stand, I sat down beside Verny and ate my lunch—what he couldn't get me to give him; he was fair, he hadn't eaten more than his share, but every time I'd fish something up out of the knapsack, he'd say, "Hey, you really want that? I'll eat it if you don't want it." After that we helped Mom and Mrs. Weeks at the stand, cleaning up out back and rearranging stuff, and then they let us sell some to people who stopped. So we had a good time all afternoon till about five o'clock when Mr. Wilson stopped in his car and asked Mom if she was ready to go home.

"You go along," Mrs. Weeks said to her. "I'll shut up. John won't be here for a while yet."

So Mom and Susie and Joe got into Mr. Wilson's car. I didn't move.

"Are you coming?" Mom said to me.

"I'll walk," I said.

"Verny?" asked Mom. "You'll be late for supper."

So Verny looked at me and then picked up his 22. "I gotta go," he said. "I'll be late for supper."

So they all drove away, and I set off up the road after them, walking. I could have waited for Mr. and Mrs. Weeks, I suppose, but I didn't want to be around anybody, so I walked. Beyond Harrington's I cut into the woods, because it's shorter; the road goes down around by the river.

I didn't know what to do. I couldn't stand the thought of living with him and Mom after they got married. Anne and Mary would be there. It wouldn't be like home anymore; it'd be like living with strangers. He'd be bossing Mom around all the time.

I kicked along through the leaves. I didn't even want to think about it. I just wanted to be rid of the whole thing. I just wanted to be left alone, forgotten. I didn't care anymore *what* they did so long as they left me out of it.

But I couldn't see any way out except running away. And Verny'd been right about that—where could I go? Anywhere I went they'd find me; I'd have to get a job, find some place to stay.

24

So I slogged along, trying not to think about it and wondering what I could do, not paying much attention to where I was going, till I looked around and saw I'd wandered off the trail way up onto Vlimey Ridge. I started back down the side of the ridge toward town and pretty soon came to a huge rock slide. It looked like the whole face of the cliff had sheared off, tumbling down, rocks all heaped and broken and jumbled for seventy or eighty yards down the mountainside, the cliff jutting up behind

it, jagged and cracked. Here and there across the slide trees were growing up out of the rocks, mostly just saplings; I guess there wasn't enough dirt to hold the roots of a big tree. But way up at the top of the slide, right under the cliff, a huge, old oak tree had grown up, its branches snaking out over the rocks, its dark leaves rustling. I clambered up to it, and behind it, between it and the cliff, there was a little flat space about eight feet across, knee-deep in leaves, hidden. It was like a fort: the black branches snaking overhead, some as thick as telephone poles, gnarled, leafy, shadowy; licheny rocks jumbled up at each side where the roots had thrust them out. If Verny and me piled up more rocks, there'd be a regular stockade. Anybody attacking us would have to climb the rock slide, and we could pick them off before they got half way. In back the cliff jutted out far enough so that even if somebody crawled way out on the point of it, they couldn't drop anything down into the fort.

Boy, I thought, wait'll Verny sees this.

And then it came to me: I'd run away to here. I'd build a lean-to, hunt rabbits, pick berries and nuts. I could sneak into Bonville at night and steal stuff, escaping back to my hideout through the mist, a sack over my shoulder. Once a week Verny'd meet me after dark on the old lumber road behind Stanner's to give me the news. I'd always wanted to go live in the woods anyway. Verny and me'd even talked about it. But I'd never figured I could desert Mom and Joe and Susie. But now, heck ...

I began to clear the space, kicking the leaves together and flinging them out onto the rock slide. Every so often I'd stop to plan where I'd put stuff: a lean-to, my fireplace, my wood pile. By the time it was too dark to see anymore, I'd cleared the whole space. I set off home feeling better than I had since Verny'd asked me about Mom and Mr. Wilson on Red Mountain.

Joe and Susie were in the kitchen with Mr. Wilson's daughters when I got there, and I could hear Mom and Mr. Wilson talking on the front porch. I didn't say anything to anybody, just got myself some dinner from the refrigerator and went back out behind the shed to eat it. Then I snuck

in and went up to bed. When Mom came in later on to say goodnight to Joe, I pretended I was asleep.

But the next morning before I could slip away, she sent Joe and Susie outside and sat me down at the table and asked me what was wrong. But what could I say? That I didn't want to live with a bunch of strangers? That I didn't want someone I didn't even know bossing me around? I glanced at her, wondering if they'd already kissed a lot. But then I thought, What do I care? I won't be around much longer.

"Nothing," I said. "I just got a headache."

"I mean about yesterday. Why wouldn't you ride home with the rest of us?"

"I just wanted to walk."

She sat down at the table next to me. I was pretending to tie my sneakers. But I could tell she was watching me.

"Aren't you going to tell me?" she said finally.

"Tell you what?" I said. "I *told* you. I just wanted to walk."

She didn't say anything. I could hear the clock ticking over the sink. Then she said,

"Well, I expect I know without your telling me."

I didn't look up.

"But it can't be helped," she said, getting up. "And if you won't talk about it, you'll have to work it out yourself. Lord knows, I can't *make* you like him."

She set her coffee cup in the sink and started upstairs. But she stopped in the doorway and said, "He's a nice man, Billy. And he's always wanted sons like you and Joey."

I didn't even look up. So she went on upstairs. I sat there awhile and then got up and stuck my school notebook and a pencil and some bread and ham in a paper bag and went off to Verny's house and told him about the hideout and what I was going to do.

"What're you gonna eat?" he asked. "You can't cook. You'll starve."

He was sitting on his back porch finishing a dish of leftover chocolate pudding.

"I'll hunt," I said.

"You haven't got a gun."

"I'll get one. Come on. You want to see the place?"

It really worried him, what I was going to eat. He talked about it all the way up the mountain. By the time we got to the rock slide he'd figured it out: I'd hunt and fish; I'd store up a barrel of apples; I'd have bunches of carrots and onions and turnips hanging from the rafters; he'd smuggle me leftovers from his house; I'd have a shelf of canned goods for emergencies.

"You don't want to get snowed in up here and have to live for weeks on nothing but bark and roots and acorns."

We started up the rock slide. He stopped.

"How about water?"

I hadn't even thought of it. So we skirted around the bottom of the rock slide and followed the cliff along, looking for a spring, and pretty soon came on a place where water gurgled out from under a ledge into a little pool about as big as a washtub. We lay down on our stomachs and drank some and it was so cold it made my teeth ache. Verny said it was the best water he'd ever tasted. So then we climbed up to the hideout, and while Verny looked to see what his mother had packed for his lunch, I drew out a plan in my notebook and measured it off.

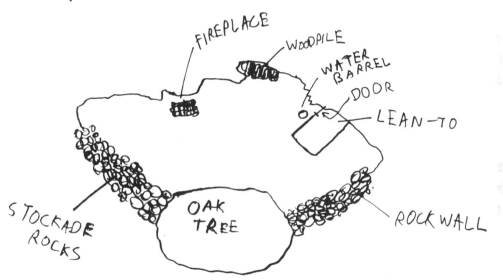

It took us almost a week to build the lean-to. We didn't just hammer some boards together like you do if you only want a place to fool around in for a summer. We spent a whole day dragging the lumber up through the woods from Mr. Bentley's scrap pile. By

31

suppertime we were all sweat and dirt; our legs were all scratched from the brambles; Verny'd cut his hand on a nail. Going home, he said it was too bad that old house was way off on Red Mountain; we could have fixed up part of that a lot easier. I said, Yeah. But it had been eerie enough for me in the daytime. I couldn't see myself trying to sleep there, the wind rattling a clapboard somewhere in the darkness, now and then the tin cans in the cellar tinkling, something scurrying in the walls.

We built the frame of the lean-to out of two-by-fours and nailed on boards and plywood scraps. I could almost stand in the end against the cliff, and the other end was set up on a wall three feet high. We left a gap for a door next to the cliff, and covered the whole thing with tarpaper and laid down strips of old linoleum for a floor. The day we finished, there was a thunderstorm, and the rain pelted down, but Verny and me sat in the lean-to as dry as two toads, the rain drumming on the roof and gurgling down the ledges.

The next day at breakfast Mom told me to be home early, the Wilsons were coming to dinner that night.

"Verny's mother's already told me I could eat at their house," I said.

But I had to give in; she said she'd call Verny's mother. And I wasn't ready to run off yet; I hadn't got a gun or my water barrel or anything. At dinner that night she sat at one end of the table and Mr. Wilson at the other. She'd cooked all day, I guess, because there was roast beef and mashed potatoes and gravy and sweet potatoes with marshmallows and string beans and turnips. After she and Anne and Mary had cleared off the dishes, Mr. Wilson came around the table and put his arm around her and said they had something to tell us. Of course, I knew what he was going to say, but I didn't care. All I could think was how stupid they looked standing up there. He was about four inches shorter, with his arm around her. It was embarrassing. Mom had tears in her eyes. I mean, you know, they were acting like teenagers. She isn't *old,* but I don't know, she had on this short-sleeved dress and her arms are sort of fat and her hair'd come loose a little and was straggling around her face.

Anyway, after he'd finished, Anne and Mary congratulated Mom and him, and then Joe asked some dumb question and they both hugged Susie and then it was my turn so I got up and kissed Mom and shook hands with him.

After dinner, while we were sitting on the porch being uncomfortable, Mom told us they were going to get married next week in the Presbyterian Church. So Joe and Susie started asking questions about the wedding, and Anne and Mary told Mom about their dresses and asked her what she thought. I sat over by the rain barrel, trying to figure how I could finish my hideout and supply it in time.

The gun was the worst problem. If I couldn't hunt, I'd never make it through the winter. But I'd figured on having a month or two to earn some money so I could buy a gun.

In bed that night Joe asked me if I thought it'd be all right, Mom marrying Mr. Wilson. I said, Sure, what could happen, Mr. Wilson was okay. I knew it wouldn't be so bad for Joe. He spent most of his time under the porch playing with his trucks. I couldn't take him along; hc was too little. The first night he'd get cold or scared and begin to cry.

So he went off to sleep, but I lay awake a long time trying to figure out some way to get a gun. Finally I decided I'd steal my father's old 12-gauge shotgun out of the trunk in the attic and sell it in Carlisle. I'd seen it once when I was helping Mom get some stuff out of the trunk. It was her fault, wasn't it? If she hadn't decided to marry Mr. Wilson, I wouldn't *need* a gun.

But when I told Verny the next day, he said I was crazy. "Nobody'll buy it. They'll know you stole it. Where would you or me get a shotgun unless we'd stolen it?"

So I said, All right then I'd steal other stuff. My father's fishing lures were up there. His tools. "We can say we found the stuff on the dump."

Verny ate some more of his bacon sandwich. He was still finishing his breakfast, but his mother'd gone over to Mrs. Ouhl's. Finally he said, Well, I could if I wanted. He guessed the stuff was part mine anyway. He'd meet me up at the hideout.

So I went back home and hung around till Mom had gone out shopping and then began to rummage through the old trunks and boxes in the attic. Pretty soon I came on the shotgun, all wrapped in greasy rags and canvas. I was tempted to take it in spite of what Verny had said, because the other stuff I was finding didn't look like it was going to

be worth much. But then I laid it aside and
went back to digging in the trunk, and right
under where the shotgun had lain, I found a
rifle, a 30-30. But that was no good to me
either—the kick's as bad as a shotgun, and
you can't shoot rabbits and squirrels with a
deer rifle, anyway. And then, under that, I
found a 25-20.

I sat back, peeling the rags off it, working the bolt. Mr. Weeks had an old 25-20 he hunted everything from woodchucks to deer with. It didn't kick much; I'd seen him shoot it . . . I poked around some more in the trunk and found three boxes of shells . . .

Finally I put everything but the 25-20 and the shells back in the trunk, locked it, and hid the key on a rafter. When I got to the hideout, Verny and me set up some toadstools and clods of dirt and pieces of bark and tried the 25-20. It did more damage than the 22, but nothing like a shotgun or a 30-30. We figured I'd just have to be more careful where I hit the squirrel or rabbit. "You'll have to aim for the head every time," said Verny.

So I could have run off the next day. I had my rifle. Verny'd lent me a lot of canned goods from his mother's pantry. I bought an old nail keg off Mr. Bentley to use as a water barrel. We figured we could haul up the other supplies later—most of the garden stuff wasn't ripe yet anyway. But Verny said I should wait till the day before the wedding. I didn't want to. I wasn't worried about anything. Everything had worked out so well. I figured I *must* be doing the right thing. But Verny said if I waited, Mom would think I'd run off just so I wouldn't have to go to the church. Then a couple more days would slide by; they'd be busy settling in and all. When they finally realized I wasn't coming back, they'd figure I must have got as far as Carlisle at least, maybe even St. Johnsbury. The State Police would search the old, boarded-up factories down by the river in Carlisle and send out an all-points bulletin and show my picture on television and Mom and Joe and Susie and Mr. Wilson and Anne and Mary, all standing on the front porch looking solemn . . . And all the time I'd be two miles away, up in my hideout, frying a rabbit or maybe training a baby raccoon I'd caught in a trap. So Verny and me spent the rest of the week nailing up shelves, hauling wood, building a fireplace, dredging out the spring.

Friday morning I crawled over Joe real quiet and pulled on my clothes. First light was just beginning to leak around the edges of the shade. Halfway down the stairs I stopped and went back to make sure I'd pulled the covers back up over him. He looked so little, sleeping all curled up, his hair mussed, that I almost figured I'd better stay. But then I remembered how Mom took him up on her lap even though he wasn't a baby anymore and always blamed me if there was a fight. So I figured she wouldn't let Mr. Wilson bother him too much and went to look in Susie's room. She'd got all mixed up in the covers like she always does. All I could see was one bare foot sticking out through the bars of the crib. As I was shutting her door, the sun came up over the ridge, and all of a sudden the whole hall was full of light. I opened Mom's door real quiet and looked in, because I knew I wouldn't be seeing her for months, maybe even years, till she was as old as Verny's grandmother maybe and I was in the army or something. She was up already, sitting at her dresser, combing her hair out. She looked around when the door squeaked.

"Why are you up so early?" she said.

"I'm going with Verny and his father to Carlisle." I wasn't, of course, but Verny was, so she wouldn't find out till it was too late.

"The rehearsal's at five," she said. "You make sure they're going to be back by four before you go."

I nodded and started to duck back out.

"And Billy," she said, turning all the way around, "I don't want to see you sulking anymore. Things may not be just to your liking, but I think I've done the best I could for everybody. I can't think about just one person. I have to think about Joe and Susie, too."

So then I didn't care whether I *never* saw her again, because she was lying: the only person she was thinking about was *herself*. Joe and Susie didn't care. *They* hadn't asked her to marry Mr. Wilson. She was just thinking about *herself*. And I was going to tell her so, but I figured she might keep me in all day if I did, so I just said, Yeah, and left. The last thing I saw of her she was turning back to the mirror.

I walked out of Bonville the opposite way so as to throw off anyone who might be watching me and then circled around and waded up Scully's Creek for about half a mile and swung myself up onto an overhanging branch and shinnied along it to the trunk and jumped as far as I could out into the woods. After that I figured I was safe even if the State Police used bloodhounds to track me.

I got to my hideout while the roof of the lean-to was still shiny with dew and climbed over the stockade rocks and just stood there, looking around, the morning sunlight slanting in through the rocks, the leaves of the great oak rustling a little overhead—my lean-to, the water barrel beside the door, my fireplace and woodpile. I figured I didn't care if I never went home, it was perfect, I could live here forever—hunting and fishing and trapping. All morning I just puttered around, fixing things up. I hung my tools on the wall of my lean-to so I'd always know right where everything was, like Verny's father was always telling us to do; I piled some stones inside the stockade rocks so it'd be easier climbing in and out; I sharpened my two knives, sitting in the door of my lean-to in the sun. About the middle of the morning I opened a can of pineapple for a celebration, and for lunch I ate a couple of the hard-boiled eggs Verny'd cooked up for me the day before. Then I rubbed down the stock of my rifle with linseed oil and reamed out the barrel and went hunting.

I didn't hunt close to my hideout though. I hiked way up to the top of the ridge and then hunted down along the other side. I figured I'd better save the game close by for winter, when it would be hard walking through the snow and cold. After a while I heard a squirrel chattering down the hill aways and snuck towards it, clambering carefully over fallen trees, skirting bramble bushes, till I came to a thicket of under-brush. Beyond it I could see the top of a big old beech tree. I could hear the squirrel chattering and the leaves rustling as it jumped and scrambled about. Maybe there were even two or three squirrels, playing together. I got down on my hands and knees and crawled into the thicket. I was dead set I was going to have game for dinner my first night in my hideout. After I'd worked my way to within about thirty feet of the beech tree, I lay down on my stomach and squirmed along with my gun laid across my elbows like a commando. At the edge of the thicket I lay still, watching the tree. Pretty soon I spotted a branch jumping and jerking crazily, not like the wind would blow it, and then I caught a glimpse of a gray tail flickering among the leaves and waited and waited, till I thought my eyes were going to fall out, and all of a sudden there he was, crouching on a branch half-hidden among the leaves, a fat old gray squirrel, staring down into the tree below him, his tail flaunting. But before I could get the sights on him, he darted away. A

branch nearby jerked . . . A chattering. Silence. I waited, searching the leaves through the sights . . . Locusts chirred in the bushes around me; a crow cawed slowly by overhead. And then, suddenly, there he was again, poised, chattering, in a gap in the leaves. *Blam!* . . . He vanished; I thought I'd missed him. Then I saw leaves rustling,

branches jerking as he tumbled down
through the tree, and I jumped up and ran
in under it, coming on him suddenly in the
leaves and forest grass, on his side, his claws
still twitching.

I ejected the shell and leaned the rifle up against the tree. I was sweating; my hair was stuck to my forehead. The tree was quiet now, no chattering or rustling, only a leaf here and there stirring in a breath of wind. I didn't feel like cleaning the squirrel right away, even though I was sure he was dead, so I stuck a twig in the ground and marked where its shadow fell and then made another mark, about a quarter inch away, and waited till the shadow moved around to it. Then I unsheathed my hunting knife and knelt over him.

A flea was crawling in the fur of his belly. Or maybe it was a nit. I don't know. I touched one of his paws with the tip of my knife. He'd looked plump and sleek and bushy tailed running along the branch, but now I could see his fur was sort of ratty and motheaten. I jerked him around by the tail till he lay square on his back, wiped my knife on my pants . . . But I couldn't make the first cut. I'd watched Verny's father clean squirrels hundreds of times; it'd looked as easy as pouring water. But every time I set the point of my knife against the squirrel, I just couldn't do it, I couldn't push it down through his soft, furry skin . . .

Finally I decided I'd cut his tail off first.

So I did that. I'd cut off lots of chipmunks' tails. Then I wiped my knife on some leaves and took a deep breath . . . and I *still* couldn't do it. So I turned my head and stabbed blindly at him and then, before I had time to think about it, stuck my knife into his chest and hacked open his stomach. I had a lump in my throat as big as a potato.

After that it wasn't so bad, though I had an awful time getting the skin off his legs and finally just hacked off his front legs altogether. I kept stopping to wipe my hands on the grass at first, but after a while I didn't bother; my hands got all sticky and stained, clogged with dirt and grass and fur.

When I finished, I laid the skinned carcass on some green beech leaves. It looked stunted and naked and ugly, like some strange, weird *thing,* not like a squirrel.

Back at the hideout, I tied a fish line around it and hung it on the two-by-four jutting out over the door of my lean-to. Then I sat down by the water barrel to rest, watching the carcass spin gently around in the sunlight . . . and all of a sudden jerked awake, my neck stiff and the shadows of the stockade rocks thickening across my hideout, flies crawling all over the carcass.

I grabbed it down and slipped and slid

along the rock slide and scrubbed it in the
spring. Then, while the fire was blazing up,
I spitted it on a steel rod Verny and me had
found in the scrap pile behind Archer's
garage. But I had an awful time cooking it.
First the rod got so hot I had to drop it, and,
sucking my fingers, look around for something to hold it with while the carcass

charred and smoked in the crackling fire. Finally I just pulled off my shirt and used that.

And then my arms kept getting tired no matter how I shifted around. I didn't think the squirrel would ever start to cook; it just kept getting blacker and blacker from the smoke. I propped the rod on my knees, on the stones of the fireplace. Finally the carcass started to sizzle and drip; I raised the rod to look at the underside; the whole thing slid off into the flames. So I poked it out of the fire, hopping around, and picked it up in my shirt and stuck it back on the rod.

But just as I got settled down again, a wind came rustling through the oak overhead, and the smoke began to drift and blow into my face. I couldn't get away from it. It didn't matter whether I stood or crouched. I coughed and choked. My eyes teared and smarted. Waving the smoke away, I jerked the rod. The carcass slid off into the fire *again*.

So I yelled and grabbed it up in my shirt and stuck it back on the rod and flopped down on my stomach, pulling the bottom of the shirt over my head to keep off the smoke.

But just when I figured the thing was

about done—it was really sizzling and dripping, all crisp and juicy in the places where soot and ashes weren't caked on it—just then the wind died, and the smoke boiled straight up in a column into the oak, and the gnats came down on me so all I could do was swat and itch and slap, and then I dropped the rod and clambered over the stockade rocks and down the rock slide and kneeled by the spring, splashing and slapping till I figured the gnats had got discouraged and gone off.

I stood up and began to dry myself with my shirt, and then I remembered the squirrel and threw down the shirt and scrambled back up the slide and over the stockade rocks. But luckily, when I'd dropped the spit, it had wedged down between two stones. My roast squirrel hung beside the fire keeping warm just as if Mom had stuck it into the top of the oven at home.

So I set it on one of the plates Verny'd found in his cellar and took out my knife and salted and peppered it and fell to. At first it tasted awful, just char and grit and ashes, but I scraped away and scraped away with my knife and pretty soon got down to the pink meat and then, geez, I figured I'd never eaten anything tastier or sweeter or juicier. I ate it right down to the bones. When I got done, there wasn't anything but a little pile of gnawed bones on the plate— along with a heap of charred and gritty parts that I couldn't eat. I sat back against the lean-to, all soaked and smeared and sooty and smudged and bitten . . . and grinned. I couldn't do anything but grin, grin and spit. I'd shot and cleaned and eaten my first squir- rel.

But that night I woke up in the thick, hot darkness of my lean-to and lay there, wondering drowsily what had woke me . . . Something was scrabbling on the rock slide.

I reached up, real quiet, and took down my rifle and laid it across my chest. But I couldn't bring myself to load it; I was scared whatever was coming across the slide would hear the bolt click and know I was awake. So I lay there in the darkness and the hot smell of tarpaper, steadying myself, listen- ing to the scrabbling, and then slowly, slowly slid open the magazine, slipped a bullet in, and biting my lip, flat on my back, eased the bolt shut.

I crawled out of my lean-to. The night

was as dark as a mine. Overhead the leaves of the oak tree rustled quietly. The thing kept scrabbling and scrabbling on the rock slide. I couldn't tell what it was. A bear? A wolf? Suppose a maniac had escaped from the insane asylum in Carlisle? And now he was crawling up the rock slide toward me. I began to tremble and swear at myself under my breath. The one thing Verny and me had forgot was a flashlight. And I could have had one so easy; there was over three dollars just sitting behind me in a tin box in the lean-to.

Way off in Bonville I could hear a couple of dogs barking. The scrabbling didn't seem to be getting any nearer. I peeked up over the stockade rocks, but I couldn't see anything in the darkness; it was like I was blind, there wasn't even a star in the sky, just the leaves rustling now and then overhead and my heart thumping and the rough rock under my hand.

I crouched down behind the stockade rocks, trying to figure out what I should do. I didn't dare try to make a run for it, not till I knew what was out there. Still, I didn't want whatever it was to corner me in my hideout either.

Finally I figured I had to make a torch somehow. Otherwise I couldn't even see to shoot if the thing started over the stockade rocks.

I crept around in the pitch darkness, one ear cocked to the scrabbling, feeling for a stick and the tar pot and my shirt. Then I crawled into my lean-to and tied the shirt on the stick and daubed it all over with tar and then pulled my blanket over my head and lit the torch, blowing on it to get it started, choking in the oily smoke. I wanted to have it going a little, so I could see something, before I let the thing on the rock slide know what I was doing. Suppose it made a rush for me? I wanted enough light to shoot by anyway.

Then all of a sudden the torch blazed up, singeing my eyebrows, and I flung off the blanket and ran outside, my rifle in one hand, the flaming torch in the other, and peered down over the stockade rocks onto the rock slide.

At first I couldn't see anything but jumping shadows, the torch blazing smokily over my head, but then I made out two small dark lumps about halfway up the rock slide. I raised the torch higher. Geez, it was two big old raccoons, gazing dumbfounded up at me. And then I remembered that after supper I'd heaved the squirrel bones and trash out over the stockade rocks. So I grinned to myself and began to call to the raccoons and sass them, till I thought suddenly, Heck, if anyone's awake in Bonville, they'll see my torch on the ridge and come up here tomorrow to find out what was going on in the middle of the night. So I stuck the torch in the fireplace and heaped dirt and ashes on it till it smoldered out. Then I threw rocks at the raccoons till I heard them scrabbling away and crawled back into my lean-to.

But lying there in the dark, I couldn't help thinking, Sure, raccoons . . . but that doesn't mean *right now* there isn't a wolf sniffing along the outskirts of the rock slide. Or a maniac limping slowly through the woods. Maybe he'd seen my torch glimmering through the trees, heard me yelling at the raccoons.

I rolled over on my side, yanked my blankets up around my head. What was I acting so *stupid* for? Here I was, way up on Vlimey Ridge, worrying about someone jumping on me? *Wolves.* I'd slept in the woods before.

But I couldn't fall asleep. I kept turning on my back, on my side, scrounging my blankets around. Then I'd lie still, listening to the night sounds outside my lean-to, telling myself to stop acting like a little kid. I wouldn't have been as scared if there'd been even a *little* light, a few stars or something. But it was *thick* dark; I couldn't see my hand before my face; I couldn't make out where the door was except by feeling along the wall.

Finally I gave up trying to sleep and hunched up in a corner, crosslegged, my rifle across my knees. Now and then I dozed off. An owl hooted up on the ridge. Once I heard the rustle of wings as something glided past overhead. Just when I thought I couldn't last any longer, I began to make out the lines of the door and then the dim shape of the water barrel and so I crawled out, stiff and sore, and leaned against the stockade rocks, shivering, watching the gray light well up in the woods and then the dawn turn the sky orange over the eastern ridge. When I could look back and see the fireplace and the lean-to, my water barrel squatting beside the door, I unloaded my rifle and crawled inside and pulling my blankets over my head, went to sleep.

About noontime Verny stuck his head up over the stockade rocks. I was squatting by the fireplace making torches.

"You look like a savage already," he said. "What happened?"

I straightened up and looked at myself. I'd cut my pants off at the knees that morning so I'd have cloth to make the torches. My undershirt was torn. I was smudged with soot, smeared with grease and mud and tar. I felt my hair; it was all tangled and cruddy.

"Yeah," I said, wiping my hands on my pants.

"You'll freeze with no shirt," said Verny, climbing in over the stockade rocks.

"Naw," I said. "Nights I'll wrap a blanket around me like an Indian. Besides, my skin's getting tough already."

I really thought it was. I didn't feel any cold at all, not even when the wind blew.

"You'll freeze," he said. "What'd you have for dinner last night?"

"Squirrel," I said, just as if it was nothing special.

While I told him about it, he helped me finish the torches, and then we ate the lunch his mother'd packed—chicken-salad sandwiches and blueberry pie and chocolate

fudge and a bottle of orange soda—and he went off, because he was going to Mom and Mr. Wilson's wedding with his mother and father that afternoon.

I cleaned up and then took my gun and hunted up over the ridge, but I couldn't get my mind off the wedding, wondering what they were all doing and what Mom thought about my running off . . . if they'd send out search parties to look for me . . . and so I kept tripping over rocks and branches, blundering along, and finally gave it up and went down to the dump behind Bentley's and filled a sack with tin cans and spent all afternoon stringing up an alarm system on the rock slide. But when it got to be five o'clock, the time of the wedding, I couldn't even keep my mind on that. So I opened a can of peaches and sat in the door of my lean-to, eating them and thinking, Well, maybe I should go after all and turn up in the church door ragged and smudged and half-naked, and everybody'd turn around and stare at me, and Mom would hug me and ask me if I was all right, and why I'd run off, and . . .

. . . and it was all crud. I set down the can of peaches and wandered around my hideout. They probably wouldn't even think of me. Why should they? I sat in the door of my lean-to, hating them and myself and everybody I could think of. The shadows of the stockade rocks stretched longer and longer across my hideout. Pretty soon the can of peaches with the spoon in it was just a dark blob on the dirt, and I glanced up and the last glimmer of the sunset was touching the leaves at the top of the oak, and then it was dark, stars winked out in the sky, and I crawled into my lean-to and pulled my blankets over me and went to sleep.

The next morning it was raining when I woke so I just lay there, listening to the drumming on the roof and the gurglings and drippings, and I didn't care about anything. I didn't care if I starved. I knew Verny wouldn't come. But I didn't care about that either. I'd start to think of what everybody would say if I suddenly appeared in the kitchen door, dripping wet, and . . . And then I couldn't think about it anymore, it all seemed like crud to me. Who'd care if I went home? Joe and Susie would be under the porch probably; Mom would be off somewhere with Mr. Wilson; Anne and Mary wouldn't care. Why should they?

They'd be washing up the dishes or something. "Oh, you're back. Your mother said you'd come back." But even that was all crud. Because what did I care what happened? Nothing would happen. And I didn't even care about that. I didn't care if suddenly everybody in the whole world began to die of something, and all over, on all the roads, you'd see people lying dead, their clothes rotting . . .

And even that was all crud, because nothing was going to happen.

So I lay all day in my lean-to, with the rain drumming on the roof, dozing off now and then, getting up once in a while to pee or try to eat something. I was afraid if I didn't I'd get sick, not that I cared, but it scared me to think of lying there sick, too weak to move—pretty soon I'd hear something scrabbling over the stockade rocks, but I'd be too feeble even to reach down my gun so I'd just lie there, pale, my eyes bloodshot, listening to the thing snuffling around outside. And then, suddenly, there'd be a gray wolf looking in the door, and he'd paw at my foot to see if I could still resist, and then drag me by the ankle up over the stockade rocks and . . . And all that was crud, too.

So I lay there, dozing, the rain pattering on the roof, dripping down the ledges outside. Then the gray, dull, rainy-day light began to fade, sucking out of the corners of the lean-to. The dripping ledges faded. The outline of the door vanished. And it was night again. I rolled over under my blankets and ground my fists into my eyes. I felt so bad I wondered if I was dying.

In the middle of the night I woke up, and the rain had stopped, and I was so cold my teeth were chattering. So I got up and wrapped my blankets around my shoulders and ran up and down under the stars to get warm. After a while my tin-can alarm system began to rattle and clatter. I lit a torch. A big old porcupine was bumbling across the rock slide, knocking against the tin cans. So I took the long stick I'd cut for a flagpole and climbed over the stockade rocks and began to chivy the porcupine, turning him every time he tried to run off, shoving the pole under him and levering him over on his back. After a while he just stopped and looked at me, shuffling around to keep his beady red eyes on me as I walked around him. So I let him shumble off into the woods.

By that time the sky was graying in the east. I got my gun and went up on the ridge to get an early start hunting, leaving a note for Verny to say I'd be back by noon. But when I got back—empty-handed again—he still hadn't turned up. I sat around all afternoon waiting for him, wondering what was the matter, what had happened at the wedding. Maybe they'd called it off, for all I knew. Anyway, I wanted to know what was going on. Besides, I was using up my canned goods too fast; I had to get Verny to bring me food till I'd learned to hunt better. So I fooled around all afternoon, waiting for him and thinking how he'd probably forgotten me and was sitting on his back porch right now, whistling and eating a piece of pie. After supper—cold corned-beef hash and some more peaches—when he still hadn't come, I decided I'd better sneak down into Bonville and find out what was going on.

I waited in the edge of the woods near the Stanner's old cowbarn till it was dark and then ran across the road and circled around to our backyard. The kitchen was dark, but I could see light glimmering at the edges of the door to the living room, so I sneaked along the side of the house through the bushes and peeked in the window near the fireplace. Mom and Mr. Wilson were watching TV. Mom was sewing, and Mr. Wilson was drinking a can of beer. I crouched down in the bushes to wait for them to say something. I could hear horses galloping on the TV and men yelling, and then a lot of shooting, and then quiet, and then some more shooting. Every time there was shooting, Mr. Wilson would say something about the guns, like "You couldn't hit a *barn* at that distance with one of those old Colts." Then the music welled up, and I heard a chair scrape, and all of a sudden, silence.

"Time for bed, Katie," Mr. Wilson said, glancing out through the front curtains.

Mom began to gather up her sewing. Then she stopped and said, "Dick, I'm worried about Billy. Suppose he isn't just up in the woods? Suppose he's gone off to Carlisle or somewhere?"

So Mr. Wilson told her she'd said herself that the Stillwell boy knew where I was. Look at the way the boy was acting, disappearing for two or three hours at a time, his mother said, and then coming out with those wild stories when he was asked where he'd been; stealing food right off the dinner table. There wasn't any doubt about it; I was somewhere up in the woods, hiding out.

"But it's so dark and cold out there," Mom said. "It rained hard all last night."

"He probably slept in someone's barn," said Mr. Wilson, locking the front door. "He can take care of himself."

So Mom started out to the kitchen with Mr. Wilson's beer can and a plate with some crumbs on it, but turned in the doorway and said, "You're sure it's right to let him defy us like this?"

So Mr. Wilson put his arm around her and said,

"Now Katie, it wasn't him that got married. It was us. We were the only ones that *had* to be there. He's got to have time to do it in his own way. I used to run off two or three times a year when I was his age. After I'd got everything settled in my own mind, I'd come back."

Then they went off into the kitchen and the last thing I heard, Mom was saying, "Yes, but he's not like you, Dick, he's . . ."

I didn't go back around to the kitchen window. I went off to Verny's house to see if he was still up; maybe I could figure a way to get him to come out without his parents knowing it. I didn't blame him for giving me away. I figured it hadn't been his fault really. From what Mom and Mr. Wilson had said, he'd tried. I don't know, I just didn't know *what* to think. About anything. I was mad because Mom was talking to Mr. Wilson like that and letting him run her. What business was it of his what I did? He wasn't my father. And yet, I don't know, I wasn't *real* mad. And I didn't feel nearly as bad as I had up in my hideout the day before, when it had rained and I'd just lain around all day. I don't know. Lying in the bushes back of Verny's house, which was all dark, I didn't know what to think about anything.

A light come on upstairs. The hall. Then the light come on in his room. His mother was leaning over his bed. Pretty soon she straightened up and began to shake something in her hand, but I couldn't tell what it was till I recognized the jerky motion: a thermometer. Verny was sick. I'd never get him out now.

So I started back to my hideout. Once I got into the woods all I could see were the trunks of trees silhouetted against the dark sky and once in a while a hazy star; underfoot I couldn't make out anything. I kept groping along from tree to tree, tripping over roots, stopping now and then to clean the cobwebs off my face. Pretty soon it seemed like it was getting darker. I couldn't see the trees against the sky anymore. Floundering along, I began to worry I'd get lost. I couldn't see anything except back down the hill through the woods, a few lights shining here and there in Bonville. Then it began to rain, softly at first and then harder, the thunder rolling and rumbling in the distance. The woods would light up for an instant, and then everything would sink back into the darkness, the rain rustling down. So I turned and floundered back to Bonville and crawled up into the loft of our shed and went to sleep in a heap of hay and old rags, the rain drumming on the roof, the thunder rumbling and mumbling away over the mountains toward St. Johnsbury. I figured I could slip out at the first glimmer of dawn, before anyone was up.

But the next thing I heard, Mom said, "Joe, you stop that. Sit up in your chair."

So I climbed down the ladder and peeked through a crack, and there was Mom at the kitchen sink, and I could see the top of Mr. Wilson's head at the table. And then I smelled bacon frying, so I figured they were all at breakfast. Pretty soon Mom went and sat down, too, and I couldn't hear anything but murmurs, but then she came back to the sink and asked Mr. Wilson what he wanted for lunch, and he told her, I guess, but I couldn't hear what he said. Anyway, she began to make it, moving about from the sink to the refrigerator, now and then reaching up to get something out of a cupboard. After a while Mr. Wilson came out on the back porch without his shirt on, just his trousers and T-shirt, and stretched and yawned, gazing up at the mountains, and then Susie came out and stood beside him, leaning up against him.

So I slunk back into the horse stall in the back of the shed and scrounged in behind the harness and waited there, with my chin on my knees, till I heard Mr. Wilson's car start up and go off. Then I slipped out the back door of the shed and through the drizzly, sopping woods to my hideout, which looked cold and miserable and uninhabited when I got there, the rain dripping off the roof of my lean-to and all my firewood soaked through.

I ate some more cold corned-beef hash, thinking about the smell of the bacon frying back home, and then I cleaned my gun, though I knew there wasn't any use going hunting till the rain had stopped. I picked up a little around the fireplace and refilled my water barrel, lugging it on my shoulder up the rock slide, and then I had more hash for lunch and dozed off awhile and thought how it was even duller in the woods when it rained than at home. I figured Verny wouldn't come because he was sick and all, his mother'd never let him out. But then just as I was deciding to go up on the top of the cliff to see what was happening down in Bonville, he stuck his head over the stockade rocks and said, "That alarm system's no good. I snuck right through it."

"It's for nights. When it's dark. D'you bring anything to eat?"

So he sneezed and then handed me a paper bag from under his slicker. When I looked in it, I thought at first he'd brought the garbage by mistake. Everything was all jumbled together: fried chicken, a wedge of cheese, some slices of bread, a lamb chop falling out of some tinfoil, an apple, a jar of leftover tunafish salad.

"I brought everything I could," he said. "I didn't have much time. I had to slip out while my mother was over at Mrs. Ouhl's. I'm sick."

He blew his nose and then he sneezed and began to cough.

So I said I knew he was and told him about sneaking into Bonville, and then he started to tell me about Mom's wedding, but I said I wasn't interested, so he told me about Mom and Mr. Wilson coming over to his house to see if he knew where I'd gone. But he kept calling Mom, Mrs. Wilson.

I had to think every time he did it: Mrs. Wilson? It sounded like some stranger. I couldn't get used to it. I tried it on myself: Billy Wilson, William Wilson, William Whitson Wilson, WWW. Not that I was going to let them change my name . . .

"You ain't listening," said Verny. He blew his nose.

"I am so. What's the matter?"

"I said I was going."

So I walked back with him most of the way, because I thought I'd try fishing in Sprout Creek. The rain had stopped, the fish would be biting. If I was going to stay in my hideout much longer, I'd have to begin getting my own food. I couldn't depend on Verny all the time.

But as I came around the bushes out onto
the bank above Stanner's, I fell right over
Mary Wilson and some boy—I suppose it
was Jimmy Stanner, because that's who she
went out with all that winter. They were
lying on the grass, kissing. I jumped up.
They scrambled apart.

"It's Billy!" yelled Mary.

I lit out around the bushes. Halfway
across the field I glanced back, and she was
coming after me, so I dropped my fishpole
and stuff and headed for the woods, but

geez, I never knew a girl could run like that. Just as I reached the wall, she grabbed me, panting, and pushed me down.

"Wait," she said.

"I'm not going back!" I yelled.

"No," she said. "I just want to talk to you. Wait."

So we both sat down in the weeds by the wall and got our breaths back, and then she said, "You're not coming back ever?"

I didn't say anything.

"Because of my father?"

I shrugged. It was her father after all. She probably liked him. So I didn't want to say anything against him. Besides, I didn't have anything against him except he'd married my mother. So I shrugged.

"Are you scared of him?" she said, slapping a mosquito on her knee. She had on shorts and a shirt and no shoes. Maybe that was why she'd run so fast. I'd never seen a girl run that fast before.

I shrugged. I didn't know what to say to her. Maybe I *had* been scared of her father, just like you're scared of anybody you don't know. But I wasn't anymore.

"I was worried about your mother at first," she said. "I thought she might try to tell me what to wear and who I could go out with. She acts sort of stern most of the time. But I guess it's just her way. She hasn't tried to boss Anne or me around yet."

"Yeah," I said.

So we sat for a while, looking out across the field.

"Were you scared of things like that with my father?" she said after a while. "Like he wouldn't let you talk to your mother? Or he'd make you work all the time?"

"I don't know," I said. "I guess I just

didn't see why Mom wanted to get married."

"Didn't she used to get lonely?"

I shrugged. I'd never thought about it.

So we sat some more, and then she asked me if I remembered much about my father, but I don't. When I was little, he was away most of the time and then he got sick and was in the hospital a lot. I remember once he lifted me up to a lion's cage at a carnival in Carlisle and another time I stayed all alone with him and my aunt while Mom was in the hospital having Joe. I asked Mary when her mother had died, and she said five years ago and told me a little about her.

So we sat some more, and then she got up and brushed off the seat of her shorts and asked me if I was coming home soon.

I said, I don't know, probably.

So she said goodbye, and walked off through the meadow and then began to run, and disappeared into the bushes. But she didn't run as fast as she had chasing me.

I collected my fishpole and stuff and went back to my hideout and sat down to think, and pretty soon I heard thunder rumbling way over toward Carlisle and it rumbled closer and closer and drops began to patter on the leaves overhead and a couple plopped onto my arms and the back of my neck, and I heard the wall of rain rustling and pattering down over the ridge, and then the storm was overhead, crashing and rolling and pelting down. So I scrambled into my lean-to to wait it out, but after the thunder had moaned and grumbled its way off over the ridges, the rain settled down to a steady pour, and it didn't look like I'd be able to hunt or fish or even light a fire for a week. I knew Verny's mother'd be keeping a close watch on him after he'd sneaked out that afternoon with a cold. So I scratched the bites on my neck and looked at the few cans still sitting on the shelf, and then wrapped my gun up in my blankets and slogged off towards Bonville.

When I came around the shed, Joe was sitting in the big rocker on the back porch, rocking and watching the rain drip off the porch roof. But he stopped rocking when he saw me. And then, "Mom!" he yelled. "Mom!" tumbling off the rocker and scrambling toward the kitchen. "Mom!" The screen door banged behind him and I heard him yelling, "Mom! Billy's out back!"

So I waited and pretty soon Mary came through the kitchen and looked out the back door. I was waiting under the apple tree.

"Hi," she said. "You coming in for dinner?"

So I shrugged and started toward the house.

"What have you got in the blanket?" she said.

"My gun."

We went inside and I laid the whole bundle on the kitchen table.

"We're in the living room," she said, "cooking hot dogs in the fireplace. We couldn't have a picnic outside because of the rain."

I looked down at myself. I'd been out in the woods for four days straight, climbed up and down the rock slide about a thousand times, daubed mud on my mosquito bites, lain around my lean-to, cooked the squirrel. I hadn't washed except accidentally when it had rained or I was slopping water up in my hands to drink. I still had on the pants I'd cut off to make torches with, and my same sneakers and socks.

"I guess I ought to wash my hands first," I said.

"Well," she said, "if you think it'll do any good."

And then she grinned at me, so I grinned back, and she pushed open the door and we went down the hall and into the living room.

Joe was watching for me.

"Hey, *Billy!*" he crowed. "Boy, are you *dirty!*"

Susie and Anne just stared. Mom looked around from the fireplace.

"Well," she said, "you're back. Come here."

Mr. Wilson was kneeling beside her on the hearth, tending the hot dogs on the grill. He glanced around at me and then turned back to the grill.

I went over to Mom, and she brushed my hair off my forehead so she could look at me, and turned me around, and then said,

"Well, you look all right."

"Yeah," I said. "I'm okay."

So then Mr. Wilson reached a hot dog on a bun around to her, and she gave it to me, and we all ate supper, nobody saying much except Joe, who kept whispering to me, "Geez, Billy, you're dirty as a *horse*" or "Mom, he's dirty as a old *sow.*"

Afterwards Mom took me upstairs and

gave me a bath, something she hadn't done for a long time. She kneeled down right beside the tub and soaped and scrubbed me. Then she combed my hair and waited while I put on my pajamas and then tucked me in beside Joe—I guess Mary had put him in—and stood there a minute beside the bed, looking down at me.

"Well," she said. "I'm glad you're back."

"Yeah," I said.